COZY
IN THE
COUNTRY
OVER
Christmas

Bethany Phelps Lepretre

Cozy in the Country Over Christmas
By Bethany Phelps Lepretre

Contact Bethany Phelps Lepretre

https://authorbethanyphelpslepretre.my.canva.site/authorbethanyphelpslepretre/

Instagram: @authorbethanyphelpslepretre

Cover Art and Character design: Keri Drechsel, @keridoodles

To my real life Memaw and Pepaw.
Thanks for always believing in me.

"To our little grown up writer- Fill this book with your wonderful stories and poems and songs. Your imagination can take you to wonderful, magical places. Never stop using your gift, for it is a gift from God. We love you so much,
   - Memaw & Pepaw Myers". (Christmas, 2003)

Table of Contents

Prologue

Seven Years Old

Laynie was going to marry Jude.

She decided this morning. She asked him if he wanted to play husband and wives with her.

 "You be the husband and I be the wife. We'll get married and have five dogs, two cats, and four kids. All girls. Two sets of twins."

She reached out to grab his hand, wanting to pull him all the way over to her grandparent's house, and away from his parents property across the road. Husbands and wives are supposed to live together.

His already wide eyes just about popped right out of his head- and off he ran back towards the safety of his parents' house.

"Wait! I'll let you name one... of the dogs!" Laynie hurried after the boy she set her sights on marrying. She was a quick runner after all. He wouldn't get too far.

Twelve Years Old

Jude's hands were sweating. Could she tell? Could she hear his heartbeat racing? He sure could. He cast a quick glance at their joined hands, trying to spot if he could physically see the sweat racing down his palms. Because if he could see it- Laynie definitely could feel it.

They had hung out and played as friends every summer and family vacation of hers he could remember. But this was the first time things were changing. They were kind of on a date. Well, at least as much of a date as possible with Laynie's Pepaw glaring daggers across the bonfire at him.

"Boy- I know where you live. If you mess with my monkey's heart, you know what's coming for you." Pepaw pointed over at the paddles hanging on the wall. One was a yellow heart shaped pillow hanging from a thin wooden handle- Memaw's Paddle. Next to it was the more gruesome of the two- a wooden plank with nails protruding from it-Pepaw's Paddle.

Jude gulped. He knew that Pepaw was like his own grandpa, but he also knew he would do something to pay him back if he messed this up. Most likely to do with animal droppings-cleaning them or eating them. Pepaw was unpredictable like that.

He dropped Laynie's hand at the memory of the threat from just an hour before, wiping his sweaty palms on his pants leg of his jeans. He looked up at her just in time to see a look of hurt flash across her face, then defiance. Good ole Laynie, never down for long.

She huffed across the bonfire and grabbed two more marshmallows, practically throwing one at him. She then snatched his hand right back. They both now only had one hand to roast marshmallows with, but neither one dropped their hands again. No matter how sweaty they got.

Nineteen Years Old

Laynie looked across the table at Jude. His hazel eyes crinkling back at her, smiling as all the Christmas lights flash around him. She loved that Memaw put them up at thanksgiving this year. Just cause she knew Laynie was coming for fall break.

Memaw is in the kitchen making Laynie's favorite- pumpkin dump cake. The smells reach Laynie all the way to the table and the TV roaring in the living room makes it impossible to hear anything. Pepaw likes to crank it and use subtitles, which just makes it feel more like home.

Freshman year was tough- being away from family, and away from Jude. But even just having a piece of her family here, made her heart feel whole again. Heck, half of her heart was sitting across from her, tasked with peeling the potatoes for the mashed potatoes for tomorrow. Of course he did it without complaint. Memaw asks him to do it, he drops whatever he's doing and says- Yes Ma'am.

Now, she can barely see her favorite smile, as its currently covered by a growing mountain of potatoes.

Huh- this is it. This is what the rest of her life could be. Happy. She'll graduate college, do a work from home job, and move back here and marry Jude. She will live across from her grandparents and be there if they need anything. Her kids will get to grow up in her favorite place with her favorite people. Perfect life. Just like her seven year old self imagined.

Chapter 1

Life really sucks sometimes.

Laynie lets out an audible groan. Why are people dumb? She used to love her at home job. Customer service rep. She's the one businesses call when they need to cover their butts after someone messes up. Instead of further endangering the company, or making a problem worse, they hire her. Dream job, right? Nope.

All she does, day in and day out, is listen to people complain, and moan and lash out at her. Regardless of the fact that she has nothing to do with the company they work for, they seem to think they can yell at her. Which she lets them, it's all apart of the job.

But two straight hours of a person cussing you out? Not okay.

She normally could let the abuse roll right off her. But ever since her Pepaw passed this summer, she just felt everything so much more. Every big feelings, good and bad, turned to tears. The bad times, she just wanted to get his advice. She wished she could just pick up the phone to hear his voice again.

Even when something good happens, which has felt less and less lately, she would remember he was gone and wasn't here to witness her happiness. Then, she would get going all over again.

Laynie pushed the laptop away from her- hoping the distance could erase what she's feeling inside.

Grabbing her iced coffee cup, Laynie took a huge gulp of gingerbread goodness. Even just the taste of Christmas Spirit, made her feel just a touch better.

Christmas has always been Laynie's favorite time of year. She has the mindset that Christmas starts November 1st, and doesn't end til after January. In fact, every year she puts off taking down the tree later and later. Last year, it was practically Valentine's Day when the last Christmas decor box was finally stowed back away.

"What do you think, Zoe?" Laynie asked her gray merle border collie. "Should we get out the tree?" Zoe looked at Laynie from her sun soaking pillow, her blue eyes solemn. They always bore right into Laynie's soul. Zoe then hid her face under her paws, letting out a single whimper.

"Yeah...I'm not ready, either. Maybe tomorrow, Zo Bo." Laynie sighed. Who was she kidding? Decorating tomorrow would not make a difference. Christmas just doesn't feel the same this year.

Leaving her office to head to the kitchen, Laynie thought of the many, many voicemails and messages waiting for her on her phone.

Probably 95% was from her mother.

Was she avoiding her mother? Not exactly. She of course came back home for the funeral. Strangely enough, Pepaw wasn't buried where most of her memories of him are, but where he and Memaw raised her mom. She made the trip back and received what felt like hundreds of hugs and "I am so sorry for your loss" sentiments. She appreciated them, but they couldn't bring him back.

Laynie came back home again for Thanksgiving, which is when the nagging, I mean nudging began.

"Laynie Marie. You need to go see your Memaw. You know I would go again, but your dad is having his dental surgery. You can't keep avoiding the farm. Your Memaw keeps saying she misses you and never hears from you. Your siblings have been three times already and you haven't gone up to see her once." So on and so forth. Laynie received voicemails and messages essentially repeating the same stuff- the mom guilt was real.

Of course, she wanted to see Memaw. She just didn't want to go back to the farm and not see Pepaw there. Her entire life, its been called "Memaw and Pepaw's farm". How could she go there without Pepaw?

But then again, Pepaw would call her a stinker for the way she has been acting lately. Or a bump on a log. Or some obscure saying he most likely made up. He always was the silliest, goofiest man in the room. He was the type to throw sugar packets from across the table at you. He would point to a spot on your shirt, only to flick your nose, "Made you look."

He wouldn't want her to sulk. In fact, he probably would be messing with her right now-"Laynie Denise-" No- that's not her name, but he had this habit of calling all the kids by the wrong name. "You haven't decorated for Christmas? It's practically spring already!"

Hearing her Pepaw's voice in her head, Laynie let out a sigh and reached to answer her ringing phone.

"Hey, Mom. Yeah, I know, I'll be there. I can leave tomorrow. Uh huh. Love you too."

Well, looks like Laynie and Zoe were heading up to the farm for Christmas after all. But first, they had some work to do.

"Come on, Zo Bo, let's get the decor out from the garage." It's Timeeeee.

Chapter 2

Laynie's Honda Civic lovingly named Hondy, that had somehow survived her entire driving career, was loaded to the brim. More Christmas decor, presents, clothes to last for weeks, and a tool kit just in case.

Plus, Laynie was not going anywhere without Zoe, so Zoe's entire collection of plushies, her kennel, her sun soaking pillow, her food and bowls, and of course, her favorite chew toy, which happened to once be Laynie's favorite slipper. Now it exclusively belonged to Zoe, no matter how many times Laynie had tried to do a swap out.

Zoe was ready to go in the back seat. Well...as ready to go as possible when she gets motion sickness <u>every single car ride.</u> Whether it was the five minute drive to the vet, or the four hour drive they were about to conquer, Zoe would be getting sick. Towels were laid across every surface area possible to prevent staining. Even though Hondy was old, she was sturdy. Avoiding barf stains was just doing the ole girl right.

With a slam of the backseat door, after making Zoe as comfy as possible, Laynie grabbed her fanny pack and got ready to strap in. She ran through her mental checklist. Gas- check. Playlist-check. Taylor queued up- check. Snacks-check. Audio book for when she is not in a jam mood-check.

She puts the car in drive and began the four hour journey. Laynie clicks shuffle on her playlist, and "Mine" comes on.

She reaches to change it out of habit. It's *their* song. She always felt the lyrics described her and Jude to a "T". Even now, years later, she can't hear that song without picturing him. His brown hair, his little scruff that appeared as they got older, but what never changed were his eyes.

Hazel with gold flecks that shined whenever he smiled. Laynie made him smile a lot. She used to live in those gold flecks, letting the warmth of his smile wash over her.

Hearing the song, she could practically still feel his warm arms around her every time he gave her a tight embrace. This song would come on the radio, and he would spin her around the kitchen floor, Memaw running to grab her camera before the moment was over.

Her hand was still frozen, right above the dial. Laynie shook herself as the song ended. She got so lost in the music, in the memories. She hasn't let herself do that in forever.

If she was honest with herself, it wasn't just Pepaw that prevented her from going back to the farm.

What used to be her prime destination spot multiple times a year, had gradually become a place she went to maybe once a year. Most of the time, her grandparents would come down to her family instead.

Laynie was avoiding him. Jude.

His parents still lived across the street, though the last she heard, he was long gone. After college. he moved up to Waco or something. Whatever. He was gone. That's all she knew.

But she always was terrified she would see him again.

She was terrified of what she would do when she would see him again. Would she slap him across the face? Would she kiss him? Would she kick him in the nuts? Would she burst into tears? Would she demand an answer for what happened to them? Would she turn the opposite direction and go running?

Probably all of the above. Maybe not in that order.

As Taylor starts yet another song, Laynie's mind starts to wander, the monotony of the road allowing her to travel through her memories.

Thinking back on her time with Jude, most were good memories. But the last few just leave a nasty stain on years of happy moments.

Another question rises to her mind- Could she ever forgive him?

Nine Years and Ten Months Earlier

"So how was your day, babe? Didn't you have a test or a project due today?" Laynie asked Jude. Their ten minute check-ins every other night were definitely hard to keep up with, but going to two different universities that felt a world apart from each other, check-ins were a necessary commitment.

"Uh. Fine, I guess." Jude mumbled. He seemed more and more short lately. The check-ins always ending because he had to rush off. He even forgot to call the other night. Laynie was trying not to stress too much about it. School never came easy to Jude, not like the farm did. He was natural there, but at school he always seemed out of place.

The silence stretched. Laynie waited. Surely he would say something else...ask how her day was? Say if he could come see her this weekend like they planned? Tell her he missed her as much as she missed him?

But he didn't do any of those things. He sighed into the receiver.

"Everything okay?" Laynie inquired, not fully sure she was ready to hear his answer. A pit of dread in her stomach fell a little deeper.

"Yeah. I'm sorry, I am just really stressed right now. Can we talk more this weekend? You still want to meet at the farm right?"" Laynie immediately relaxed- he remembered.

"Yes! Can't wait- see you then. I know school has been stressing you out lately, but I believe in you babe. I love you." She wished she could squeeze him through the phone. She could tell he needed a hug. She owes him one this weekend for sure.

"Yeah," Jude said a bit sadly, "You too."

Chapter 3

Present Day

Laynie had called Memaw to let her know she was heading in, Memaw was so excited that they were going to spend Christmas together.

"Goodness, I need to go grocery shopping!" Memaw exclaimed. In the country, grocery shopping was a whole ordeal. The best grocery store was forty-five minutes away in Buffalo. In fact, Memaw had to prepare coolers for anything bought frozen. She would always buy everything in bulk and store the excess in a deep freeze.

The deep freeze was bigger than Laynie. It was in their walk in laundry room which was practically a bedroom itself-right across from the giant walk in pantry. Laynie always was amazed as a kid of the towers of canned goods and giant tubs of crisco that lined the shelves. If any kind of natural disaster struck, Memaw's pantry was her first stop. It truly was the stuff of legends.

"Memaw, just wait and we can go to the store together. I know you're about to buy out Walmart. I can help you load everything." Laynie could just picture her little Memaw trying to lift the giant containers of all the food, probably resulting in a thrown out back. If the grocery store was far, the closest medical facility was even further.

When Laynie's best friend, Kristi, had a four wheeling accident at the farm, she had to be life flighted out since ambulances don't go this far into the country. Maybe they try to avoid dirt roads? Even then, the life flight helicopter still took forever. Even as a thirteen year old, Laynie learned that day if she ever was going to get injured, it better happen back home.

"Don't you worry about it, darlin'. I got some help here." Laynie could hear the smile in her Memaw's voice. Huh. Maybe she hired some help? That would be great if that were true. Laynie constantly worried how Memaw was going to handle an entire forty acre farm filled with ten cows, three goats, two cats, and two dogs. Well, technically only one dog, but Memaw has claimed Zoe as her own. Laynie swears Zoe would leave her for Memaw, especially given the freedom to run around and chase squirrels all day.

Laynie knew Pepaw would do so much-even probably when he shouldn't have. He was the type who believed in hard work. Honestly other than her own dad, she only knew one other person with that mentality. She hadn't seen him in years, so who knows if he even still acted like that. Laynie liked to think she gained that trait as well, but the thing with Laynie is once her mind is made, that's all there is.

Graduated college in three and a half years, done solely to prove to herself that she could. Moved into a solo apartment right out of college, even against the advice of a family friend financial advisor, who she wanted to prove wrong with every fiber of her being. Became vegetarian for a quick diet change up, but stayed one for ten plus years after hearing all the haters try to change her mind.

Laynie was unapologetically her own person. Yes. Stubborn is another word for what she is. Determined is her choice of phrasing though- better connotation.

Her determination helped her with her job too. Not many people could handle dealing with people all day- even through a screen. But she actually was really good at her job-normally. She is compassionate, but firm, and will not let people walk over her, including some big businesses that in the past tried to pay her less that what she was worth. Laynie just stood her ground- "You need me, I however, do not need you. If you meet my financial requests, great, if not, also great, but I walk away. It's completely up to you."

That was a meeting she attended in person. She wanted them to know how serious she really was. Her Dad just laughed when she told him about it after wards.

"They never stood a chance. Stubborn little princess." A grin coming through on his face as he patted her on her back, heading towards the den. If anyone else other than her dad called her that, it might be offensive to her. But with him, it was probably closer to the truth than she cared to admit.

The drive was right under four hours this time, or three Taylor Swift albums and two chapters in her audiobook- whatever is your preferred unit of measurement.

Laynie knew she was close when the roads turned to a red dirt. She turned right onto a tunnel of trees, light shining through sporadically whenever there was a gap in the leaves. She spared a look in her rearview at Zoe, hoping the poor pup wasn't feeling too sick. But the silky soft old pup seemed to know they were close. Her dark grey ears were perked and she was alert, unlike she had been for the majority of the trip.

They passed the dilapidated trailer that her family used to joke to newbies was the 'general store'. It was home to probably raccoons, coyotes, and deer. Never once had it actually been a general store-but it was always fun to see people's eyes widen thinking they were going shopping amongst the critters.

Then, as Laynie made the final turn, her second home came into view.

The house was a ranch style home- with mixed brick of reddish hues, the wooden beams painted red and the wrap around porch that went around the majority of the house. There were rows of crops in the garden by the side of the house- which made every meal taste better, knowing you had picked the vegetables yourself. Pepaw used to eat things straight from the garden, without rinsing it, much to Laynie's disgust. "It'll give you hair on your chest, monkey. Then, you'll be purdy just like your Pepaw." Laynie smiled as the memory faded, pulling into the carport.

She hopped out of the car, barely putting it in park due to her excitement. She had been dreading this trip, but now that she was here, she felt like she was home for the first time in months. Laynie felt tears come to her eyes. She could feel him here. She thought being here would make it worse, but she feels closer to him than she ever did moping around her apartment.

She quickly let Zoe out, letting the sweet pup get her sea legs again. Zoe went to go to the bathroom, then fully got the zoomies. Laynie smiled as Zoe sprinted back and forth from fence to the car, back to the trees, and back to the car, waiting for Laynie to lead the way inside.

Laynie grabbed all her goodies- luggage, Zoe's bag, and Christmas decor for Memaw, and piled it on her body, it towering and covering her line of sight.

Hoping Zoe didn't shuffle in front of her feet, Laynie made her way to the creaky screen door, knowing each step towards it by heart.

Creakkkkk. The trusty door sung for her as she opened the door with a free foot. Sensing a presence, Laynie shuffled in through the door.

"Hey, Memaw! Can you give me a hand? I may have gone a bit over board bringing decorations this time."

A deep voice cleared its throat. "Ahem. Not Memaw."

Laynie just about pissed herself, and she did drop every thing that was jengaed perfectly in her arms. She tensed, waiting for the crash of ornaments and glass figurines to reach her ears. But it never did.

She opened her eyes that she had squeezed shut. The crash never happened. Because Jude was there and caught it all.

Jude was *there*. Laynie stared in shock at the man in front of her, restacking all of her things and organizing them on the table. All the while avoiding eye contact with her.

"How does he somehow look better? Ten years apart had done him good. Grr. Laynie-control your thoughts." Laynie's brain was going ninety miles a minute. How was he here?

Jude looked the same, but better. He had filled out more, wearing his typical flannel- the uniform of the country boy. He had his work boots on, and he had some scruff on his face, which only made him more attractive somehow. His brown hair in the same haircut she had known him to have his whole life. And of course-those eyes. Hazel with gold flecks, and right now, they were suddenly locked on hers, sheepishly.

"What. The. Hell. Are. You. Doing. Here." She spit each word out, making each one its own sentence. He averted his eyes, as if he couldn't stand to look at her.

Memaw came in right then from the garage door connected to the kitchen. As if sensing the awkwardness, she pranced over to Laynie and wrapped her arms around her. Giving her a peck on the cheek, she whispered in Laynie's ear, "Manners, young lady."

Then, Memaw said out loud, "So good to see you, sweetheart! Let's get you all sorted, darlin'." She grabbed the suitcase, which Laynie reached for, not wanting Memaw to carry the devastatingly heavy bag.

"Hey there, Memaw. Good to see *you.*" Did she emphasize the you? Perhaps. "I'm going to go unpack real quick, I'll be out in a bit." Laynie then went to the hall, calling for Zoe in her flee away from the man she used to think she was going to marry.

She spared a glance back, expecting Zoe to be right on her heels.

But the traitor was getting all the love and pets from He who must not be named.

"Judas." Laynie whispered under her breath. She then hid herself in the safety of her room. Fully prepared to hide there for the rest of time if need be. Some Christmas this was going to be...

Chapter 4

Laynie's stomach growled alerting her to the sad truth that she in fact could not hide the rest of the holidays, much less the night.

The smell of Memaw's cooking wafted through the house.

"Is that chicken and dumplings? Did she make me one without chicken?" The temptation was too great. Laynie caved and left her safe haven.

"Hey there, Laynie. Nice of you to join us. I made you your own vegetarian bowl." Laynie breathed a sigh of relief. At least her leaving her sanctuary was worth it- Memaw's cooking was like no else.

"Thanks, Memaw." Grabbing the bowl, she proceeded to try and make a quick escape to the living room, and eat her soup in peace.

"Don't you dare, young lady. 'Round here, we eat at the table." Memaw chastised her granddaughter. Laynie sighed, she had a feeling that would happen.

She sat at the chair furthest from Jude, which also happened to be the chair right across from him. Great.

"So," Wanting to tackle the elephant in the room, "Why are you here, Jude?"

Jude had been taking a sip of sweet tea, and her question made him choke, much to Laynie's secret glee.

Sputtering about, Jude reached for his napkin and wiped his chin and mouth.

Looking at his dripping mouth, Laynie instantly regretted her actions. She should not draw attention to his lips. She should not think about how perfect they used to feel on her own mouth. She definitely should not think about the hours they used to spend making out in his truck.

Memaw answered for him, "He is the help I told you I had. He has been a huge lifesaver since your...". She stopped, wiping a tear from her eye.

"How long has this been going on?" Laynie asked, not wanting to dwell too much on Pepaw at the moment.

"Well, let's see...We've been lucky to have Jude's help permanently for over the past year." Laynie's mouth dropped. The past year? So, he was there months before Pepaw died. What the actual heck? A new thought crossed her mind.

"Why weren't you at the funeral? You and Pepaw used to be so close." She asked, accusingly. He was practically another grandchild to her Memaw and Pepaw. She was even more devastated not seeing him there. She had no plans to talk to him, but she expected him there. When he wasn't, she not only was sad, but she was mad. Regardless of her own feelings towards Jude, Pepaw would have wanted him there.

He cleared his throat, finally recovered from the choking attack.

"I wanted you to have your time to grieve. I didn't want to make it about me." So, he did it for her. Great. Just freaking great.

She was stunned into silence. Luckily, Memaw took it upon herself to fill the silence. They made polite small talk the rest of the dinner. But Laynie couldn't quite get over Jude and what he had done for her. What he had probably been doing for her grandparents all this time. She risked it then, she looked at him.

His eyes were already on her, a want and a sadness seeming to come from his eyes.

But how could that be? Jude is the one that ended things. Laynie wanted to marry him, and Jude broke her heart.

The memory was still so fresh, as was the heartbreak. It's almost as if it had happened yesterday, instead of ten years ago.

They had plans to meet at Memaw and Pepaw's on their first free weekend in forever. She knew long distance was making them struggle, but she thought if they could just see each other everything would go back to the way it used to be. She was wrong.

He pulled her aside almost immediately, not even stopping to say hello to her grandparents. They went to the one spot they could talk alone, without interruption.

Right behind the main house was a small cabin, with the barest of necessities. But even as kids, it was always their escape. As they grew older, their intentions were less pure...but they still considered it their secret hideout.

The tiny cabin was older than the house, and it looked it. The walls held up enough to keep the animals out, but barely. Luckily, they had added a double screen around the exterior to help keep out unwanted guests.

Jude had pulled Laynie along all the way to the cabin. "Wow, I guess it has been a while...". Laynie thought, her thoughts going somewhere else entirely.

But when Jude finally faced her once they were inside, there were tears in his beautiful eyes.

"I can't do this, Laynie." The words sliced right through her heart.

"Can't do what?"

"This. Us. College. I am fucking everything up." He stammered, looking at his hands.

"I am dropping out," he continued. "I failed too many of my classes. I am moving back home, then I may go somewhere else...I just don't know."

'Take a breath , Jude. That's okay. We can face this together. I love you." Laynie tried to reach for his hands.

He gently pulled his hands from hers, "I cheated, Laynie. Some sorority girl threw herself at me at a party." The world stopped. Laynie couldn't breathe. He continued, "It meant nothing, and I knew it was a mistake. I wish it hadn't have happened, but it did. I can't take it back."

Laynie couldn't believe her ears. How could the one person who had always taken care of her hurt her this much?

"That's what made me realize I needed to come back home for a bit. I became someone I didn't recognize. I always thought I would never hurt you, but the person I was becoming hurt you so much. I am so sorry, Laynie. If I could take it back I would. I think I need time to figure out how I got so messed up; how everything got so broken."

"You did this." She whispered. Her voice shaking with rage. "That's how it happened. You avoided me for months, even when I tried to talk to you, asking what was wrong. You destroyed us. That's what happened."

He reached for her then, as if to pull her in his arms as he had so many times before.

She recoiled, pushing him away. "Jude, I never want to see you again, you hear me?"

She turned and stormed out of the cabin, which seemed to now be forever ruined for her. Every good memory she had here, washed away in the last two minutes.

She barely could hear on her way out the door, when he answered in his soft southern drawl, "I hear ya."

She didn't spare a glance back at the only boy she had ever loved, but if she had, she would have seen a slow steady stream of tears gliding down his face.

Chapter 5

Laynie woke up the next morning before the sun even started to rise. She barely got any sleep after the dinner last night.

Seeing Jude again after all these years just brought all of the memories right back- the good and bad. Especially the bad.

She had to excuse herself before dessert even, after getting so lost in the memory of Jude breaking up with her. Breaking her heart. Destroying all of her hopes and dreams she had of the two of them growing old together.

It took all the power she had inside to not start tearing up right there at the dinner table.

"Ughhhh." She will not let this happen again. She will not wallow like she's nineteen again. That was ten years ago, damnit. She lives on her own, has a career, and a pretty enjoyable life, for the most part.

See, this is what was keeping her up last night- comparing her current life to the life she could have had with Jude. Would they have moved to the country? How many kids would they have? Would they still be together if she had just tried a little harder?

No. That is a rabbit hole she could not and would not fall down. A relationship requires two people- it couldn't have been solely on her to save it. No matter how many times that thought ran through her head over the years.

Laynie looked around her room- the same room she has had for almost thirty years. She stayed in that bed every night she can remember for every trip to the farm. It used to be her mom's room before her mom met her dad.

Window on the front side of the room, towards the front of the house. That was the only light she ever used during the daytime- no lamps or anything til it was too dark to see. Then, the giant face toy box right below the window, slightly creepy and full of toys probably older than she was. Every sibling, cousin, and grandkid had used this toy box and added to it over the years, accumulating in a hodgepodge treasure chest of toys spanning a thirty year period.

Laynie sighed, giving up on trying to fall back asleep for another hour. She needed to distract her self, and only one thing could possibly take her mind off of the attractive country boy that was probably already about to start working outside, less than ten feet away from her...

Christmas.

Laynie decided right then and there, her main focus for the time being was making Memaw's house feel like a winter wonderland. She knew Memaw would feel Pepaw's absence now more than ever, after sixty Christmases spent together. So, Laynie was going to do all in her power to make Memaw feel the Christmas spirit, even if Laynie herself had a hole in her own heart too.

They would help each other. The idea of Memaw's Christmas cooking made Laynie hop out of bed. Luckily, she came prepared.

She grabbed her favorite Christmas sweater, since it was starting to get Texas chilly outside- a whopping 50 degrees. It had a Santa Claus wearing cowboy boots and said, 'Merry Christmas Y'all!' She may live in the city, but she had a country girl heart.

Laynie grabbed her gingerbread latte coffee grounds from her duffel, ready to make a cozy beverage and get to work.

Zoe ran out with her, ready to go outside. Laynie let her out, trying to still stay quiet. While living on a farm normally meant early mornings, Memaw was more of a night owl herself. Pepaw was the one who used to wake up with the rooster. Now, Jude is the one who gets the morning chores done- "Nope, don't think about Jude. Only Christmas thoughts for the rest of the day, I mean year." Laynie thought, before grabbing the coffee pot to make a fresh pot of gingerbread coffee to go with her sugar cookie creamer she had also brought from home.

While waiting on the coffee, Laynie laid out a game plan for the day.

1. Drink gingerbread coffee, Christmas cheer needs fuel.
2. Tidy up a bit first, both outside porch and inside. Need a blank canvas to work with.
3. Start outside and work your way in- so outdoor lights, garland on porch railing, wreaths on doors first. Then, take care of tree inside.
4. Avoid He who must not be named at all costs.

Laynie had to start with the outdoors, so she would have light to work, but she was terrified of doing the exterior lights on the roof.

She was fully capable of using a ladder, she just happened to be a little afraid of heights.

Well, maybe more than a little. Maybe she had to take ambien every time she flew, so she never would physically see how high she was off the ground. Maybe she had passed out from fear in high school the one time her friends made her do one of those tower drop rides. Luckily, passing out made her not remember the trauma too much.

There was a definite loss of pep in her step as she walked the ladder over to the side of the house. She started giving herself a mental pep talk, "Just one light at a time, Laynie. This will be over before you know it, then you can go back to the safety of the ground." Each step up on the ladder, her heart sunk a little lower into the pit of her stomach.

String of lights in hand, Laynie closed her eyes as she took the final step of the ladder. Keeping her eyes closed, she reached up towards the edge of the roof.

"Probably not a good idea to close your eyes while standing on top of a ten foot ladder, Lay." A deep voice came from below her. She just about jumped off the ladder in shock, her fear of death the only thing stopping her.

"Do not call me that. Also, how dare you sneak up on me while on top of a ten foot ladder!" Laynie screeched, still keeping her eyes closed. The lights were still in her hand, but she was gripping the side of the ladder so hard her knuckles were white.

"Now, why on earth would someone deathly terrified of heights put themselves in the position where they are trapped on a ladder?"

She could imagine the smirk he had on his face- one side of his mouth turning up, and a glint in his hazel eyes.

"You know, just cleaning out the rain gutters. No, dumbass. What does it look like I'm doing?" Laynie responded with a sarcastic bite to her tone.

"Looks like you're trapped on a ladder. Do you need some help getting down?"

She managed to creak one eye open, not daring to look down. Took a deep breath, trying to calm her racing heart and said, "I can do it." She took the first step down, took another breath and stepped again. Good- still alive. She prepared to take another step when strong arms gripped around her side picking her up and depositing her safely on the ground.

She whipped around at him, inches away, "I told you I could do it, why did you take me down?"

"I know you *could* do it, darlin'. But you didn't have to. Anytime I get a chance to take care of you, I will." His words made her feel all hot for a second, her body betraying her. She suddenly became all too aware of how close they were standing.

She shook herself and took a few steps back, maintaining a safe distance.

He laughed to himself, that signature smirk back again, "I will take this job, Laynie. Let me do the lights, and you can start on the porch garland." She took a breath to argue but the tips of his fingertips grazed her lips, stopping her. "If you try again on this ladder, my work day will be shot spending the whole time worried about you. Do this for me, will ya?" He waited a beat, holding her eyes, before removing his fingers and turning back towards the ladder. Lights in hand, he made his way up as if it was the easiest thing in the world.

She wanted to argue, but she also wanted to live. So she did what she was asked and turned back towards the giant garland on the porch. With the porch wrapping around 75% of the house, it was quite a job in itself. Plus a job that involved both feet staying on the ground.

She could handle that.

A few hours later, just as the sun was just beginning to lower in the sky, the outdoor decor was finally done. Laynie had successfully wrapped the entire porch railing in a mix of faux garland, red bows, cranberry string, and of course white Christmas lights. She couldn't wait to see how it looked once it was completely dark, that would be the true test of her work.

Even though she did not want to, she also had to give Jude some credit. He had meticulously put up lights over every edge of the roof; there was no stone unturned. If she was honest with herself, she would not have come close to what he was able to do with the lights. It probably was a good thing he had found her with the ladder when he did, otherwise the whole thing may have ended with a lightless house and a helicopter trip to the nearest hospital.

He finally climbed down as he plugged in the last light. Now, all that was left was to plug the main power cord in to the exterior house outlet. Jude walked towards Laynie, "You care to do the honors, darlin'?"

Laynie looked at him as he stopped to her right, both surveying the work that had been put it today. This would be the test...would it still feel magical this Christmas? She felt like so much was riding on getting this right, making everything whole again for everyone. This outdoor decor was the first test.

She took a deep breath, and reached for his arm, giving it a supportive squeeze. "Go ahead, Jude. You got this." She took a breath, feeling nervous suddenly. Why did it feel like she was on a roller coaster?

Jude waited, looking back at her, ready to plug everything in. "Ready?"

"Yes" She breathed, anticipation filling her chest.

He plugged in the cord into the external outlet, lighting up the entire roof and turning on the entire lit garland as well.

The night sky suddenly shone even brighter with the glow of the Christmas lights.

The entire roof edge was glowing along with the lit garland around the porch. It was beautiful.

He returned back next to her and said, "It's magical, Laynie. You did it." She wanted to argue with him, saying she didn't do much, he was the one who did the majority of the hard stuff.

But she was speechless, for once.

Regardless of them doing it together, in this moment, she felt as if Pepaw was there. She finally felt right for the first time in forever.

A tear rolled down her cheek. Jude noticed, because instead of looking at the lights, he had been looking at Laynie.

He swiped his thumb across her cheek, wiping her tear. Then, he started walking towards the side door.

"Come on. Let's get Memaw, she'll love this."

Laynie took one more look just for herself, soaking in the perfect moment, then she followed Jude into the house.

Chapter 6

Laynie went to bed that night with a warm heart, and when she woke up early the next morning she still felt the effects. Her and Jude were working together on something, and it resulted in something truly beautiful.

Memaw's reaction to the lights was spectacular- first shock, then she gasped covering her mouth as tears started to flow down her face. She then grabbed the two of them and pulled them in for a bone shattering hug. Putting them closer together than they had been for a while...

It had been a day full of hard work, but seeing her reaction made it all worth it.

Laynie and Jude had been pure business, but there were a few moments that made Laynie question his feelings.

Honestly, him saving the day and effectively saving her in the process.

Then, there's the way he seems hyper focused on her. All day she could sense him watching her, but he would always turn his head when she would turn to check.

Maybe she was imagining things.

But then again, there was that moment before they got Memaw, that was just the two of them, staring at their handiwork. Then again, when she started tearing up and he wiped the tear from her face.

Do friends lovingly wipe away other friend's tears?

Did she want to follow up on that question? Did she truly want to explore a path with the man that broke her?

Not just broke her heart, he broke her completely. She had given everything to him, and imagined her entire life with him, only to have the entire floor ripped out from underneath her.

She shook her head, letting out a deep breath. No. She can't, she's her own person now. She can't get wrapped up in twenty year old thoughts.

Laynie looked over at Zoe who had just started whimpering at the window. Zoe looked back at Laynie, begging with her big eyes to go outside. Thing is, this wasn't Zoe's typical morning angst. She seemed truly upset.

Laynie hopped out of bed and ran out after her. Zoe flew to the back door, and scratched waiting to be let out.

Laynie reached for the knob and barely had a chance to crack it open when Zoe slivered herself out.

She took off running towards the back of the garden and Laynie rushed to follow after her pup.

Zoe ran through the garden and stopped over by the leafy greens- spinach and kale plants.

Laynie was right behind her and gasped when she realized what Zoe was so upset about.

The vegetables were shredded, as if someone had torn up everything. She looked around, the leafy greens were not the only things touched.

The potatoes had been uprooted and dug out, the apples were thrown about, bites taken here and there. Strawberries off the vine and rolling around in the dirt, all bruised and smashed.

What had done this?

But Zoe was not done. She whimpered again and brushed her paw on something just past the greens.

There was a touch of red on the greens. Laynie looked around, thinking maybe it was the strawberries. Then she followed the red.

The red went out of the garden and around the side of the house, closest to her window.

A family of dead rabbits were lying there, as if resting. But the red surrounding them made it clear, they were not sleeping.

Something had killed them.

Laynie cried out, and her hands went to her mouth in shock.

She felt strong arms come behind her, turning and pulling her into his embrace.

She felt Zoe come up and lean into her leg, her way of giving Laynie a hug. Laynie felt a few reassuring licks on her calf. Jude started circles on her back, quietly reassuring her and whispering comforting nonsense.

Laynie felt her self start to calm down, her heart rate coming back to its normal pace.

Then she heard a *chk chk* from behind them and she broke free from Jude's arms.

Memaw stood there, pjs and all, with a shotgun cocked on her shoulder.

"What kind of rascals we got over here?"

Laynie stared at her eighty year old grandmother, as she stood there with a vintage shotgun probably older than Laynie was.

Jude walked over and gently loosed the gun from Memaw's grip, unloading it and pocketing the shotgun shells, before handing it back to her. Laynie gave him a glare as he walked back over to her. "Don't worry, these were her last ones. I've been hiding them all. Just couldn't find these last ones." He whispered to her, knowing exactly what the glare was for.

He then said at a normal volume, "We got a varmint, ma'am. The crops got all tore up and dug out, and there was a family of rabbits tore to pieces right outside of Laynie's room." Laynie wanted to start crying again. Maybe she should have let Zoe out sooner...

Jude turned towards her, "This looks like it happened in the middle of the night, nothing we could have done. " He gave her a reassuring nod. Of course he knew she was already blaming herself.

"Well, hotshot, what's the plan?" Memaw asked, as she looked at her now empty shotgun. "I just lost months worth of crops, this can't keep happening. We need to stop it now."

"Yes ma'am. I have an idea." Laynie waited, assuming it would be sprinkling baking soda around the fence line or something.

"I'll stay here tonight. Keep everything safe and I will take care of it tonight."

Laynie couldn't stop herself when her mouth full on dropped at his words. Jude. Was. Staying. Here.

"But, there's no room!" She stammered out. "I am in the guest room and the other rooms are full of stuff!" Please, please, please....

"Nonsense. There's plenty of room for you in the cabin, right, Jude?" Memaw said matter of factly.

Jude looked right at Laynie before answering, "Yes ma'am. Plenty of room in the cabin."

The cabin. He was going to be in the...cabin. Where they had, and then they...and that was where he...Laynie's mind started racing, along with the quickening beat of her heart. Oh shit, this was gonna be a long day and night.

Chapter 7

Laynie tried to distract her self for what's to come. She had her gingerbread coffee, she spent hours throwing her self in decorating the inside of the house, and she even managed to brush out Zoe's long coat.

But nothing was working.

No matter how many ornaments were put up, lights and garland on display in the kitchen, or the amount of hair that came out of Zoe...she still couldn't stop thinking of tonight. Jude would be so close to her. The cabin was merely feet away from her own bed. Would she even be able to sleep tonight?

Laynie pulled her self back to her current task, baking with Memaw.

Was it even Christmas time if Memaw wasn't baking some delicious treat?

"Grab some more of the cinnamon, Laynie. I don't think we put enough in." Laynie shook some more spicy smelling goodness in. They definitely have put in enough, but Laynie would never complain about too much cinnamon in her snickerdoodle cookies. Cinnamon was one of iconic scents of Christmas time. Laynie's favorite combo was gingerbread latte and snickerdoodle cookies for breakfast.

While Laynie's main job at the moment was snickerdoodles, Memaw was getting the wassail started.

Wassail was a tradition that had always been around in Laynie's family. Every Christmas morning, Laynie demanded her mother make it. Laynie's mom would sigh and with a smile, hand all the kids an orange and a bowl of cloves.

Though wassail was amazing, to make it was kind of painful. Oranges needed to be covered in cloves, with barely any of the orange peel showing.

Everyone loved wassail, but hated the work that was put in to it. At least three large oranges were needed, apple juice, pineapple juice, honey, cinnamon, and lemon juice. Even though Memaw had made it thousands of times, she still pulled out her notecard recipe.

Laynie prepared herself, ready for the pain of pushing hundreds of cloves into oranges. "Okay, Memaw, I'm ready. Give me the tiny torture devices."

"Huh? Oh, you mean the oranges? Jude took care of that already, sweetheart. He mentioned something about knowing how much you didn't like doing it." Memaw was turned towards the stove top, already busy tossing in all the ingredients that come together to make the magic that is wassail.

How dare he? How dare that man do something just so she didn't have to do it? Didn't he realize she was trying to *not* think about him? All these sweet and thoughtful things he kept doing was making it harder and harder to remember all the bad stuff.

Maybe that was his plan all along.

Laynie now with a free evening, decided she was going to look at the work she had done today.

She poured herself some eggnog, topped it with some nutmeg, and poured in a thimble full of brandy in honor of Pepaw. He would have put in a bit more than a thimble though...

Should she grab Jude some too? He used to like eggnog. But honestly this week had been the first communication they had in ten years, he may have developed a dairy or a nut allergy since then. People do develop allergies later in life, in fact Laynie was pretty sure she was allergic to pesto. Did that mean she was giving it up? Nope. Pesto pasta was worth a rash and a couple of Benadryls.

Laynie sat on the couch in the living room admiring her handiwork and enjoying this moment of just her and her eggnog.

She looked above the brick mantle, the lucious green garland, with the string of cranberries, all lit aglow by hundred of tiny Christmas bulbs. Over to her left was the piano she had played (very badly) hundreds of times growing up. It had the same garland draped across the top, but there were picture frames that stayed up year round resting on top of the garland.

Laynie's eyes stopped on one of her Memaw's favorite pictures of her- Laynie and Jude about eight years old; Laynie had her arms around Jude squeezing him and Jude had the biggest smile on his face as he had one hand gripping her arm right back. This was when she remembered he actually started liking her as much as she liked him. Honestly, as a seven year old, she enjoyed the chase. By eight, they were best friends.

Laynie smiled at the picture, missing what used to be. Even before they started dating, they had been best friends. Her best friend of almost twenty years, gone in an instant.

She was actually surprised she hadn't seen him all day. While she had been inside, Jude had been outside, not only doing his daily chores, but doing what he could to get rid of the varmint.

Jude was pretty positive he knew what it was- a coyote. Or as they say in the country- a coyote. (Two syllables vs. three- pronounced CAY-OHT)

For Laynie, even though she knew coyotes could be mean, it was hard for her to picture basically a lanky pup destroying a family of rabbits. But, also most of her knowledge of coyotes consisted of Wile E. Coyote and the Road Runner... so, safe to say she was no expert.

Even though Laynie hadn't seen Jude, as the hours went by, he still consumed her thoughts.

She saw him for a second as he grabbed his to go plate from Memaw at dinner, he headed over to his parent's house to go pack an overnight bag to bring to the cabin.

Laynie ate her supper quietly, thinking about Jude. She said goodnight to Memaw and showered, with a lot on her mind. Or mainly... one thing on her mind.

She laid down in bed, too restless to sleep. Zoe had no such issues. She was snoring, fast asleep over on her puppy bed, no cares in the world. Laynie looked out at the window, seeing a glow from a fire outside.

He was so close.

Laynie squeezed her eyes shut. Go to sleep. Go to sleep. Ugh, not working. She kept picturing things. Things she shouldn't be picturing. Things she had no right to picture anymore.

The cabin Jude was going to stay in tonight, they used to sneak to together. Many times...

With her eyes closed, her mind went through flashes of memories.

Laynie pushed Jude against the wall of the cabin, feeling the tension of his muscular chest underneath her right hand. She remembers how she could feel his steady heart start to race as she ran her left hand on the side of his face, the short stubble tickling her fingertips.

His hazel eyes gripped hers and he gave a long appreciative look up and down, before picking her up and she wrapped her legs around his waist.

She couldn't help it- she let out a squeal.

His hands under her hips tightened as he led her over to the tiny twin bed.

She pulled away and looked him in the eye-"Don't you dare." Laynie held his stare, daring him to defy her.

"Already done, darlin'." He grinned at her before tossing her right on the bed.

Laynie screamed, followed by a series of uncontrollable giggles.

Jude let out a deep growl, his face broke out into a mischievous grin, before tackling her on the bed.

They rolled around, each one fighting the other to be the tackler. The poor bed creaking every time they rolled. Laynie finally settled on top of Jude, gripping him tight with her legs, holding him in place, right where she wanted him- underneath her.

Laynie pulled herself back to the present, now restless *and* turned on.

She sat straight up in bed, seemingly decided on what she was going to do next.

She grabbed a hoodie, put it on over her pajama top, and quickly pulled on a pair of jeans. Laynie tip toed past Zoe, not wanting to disturb the pup. Little did Laynie know, Zoe cracked one eye open and spotted her owner sneaking out the door. She then burrowed deeper into her bed, and fell promptly back asleep, not a care in the world.

Laynie quietly went through the house, making her way towards the door. She took a deep breath, ignoring her nerves, and went outside.

Jude had his back to her, still wearing his flannel, and he had a long metal stick poking the large bonfire. There was another chair set up right across from him. Laynie moved past him and claimed the chair for herself.

He gave her a smile and handed her a metal stick just like his. Then, she realized there was a big fluffy marshmallow on the end of it.

Two chairs. Two sticks. Plenty of marshmallows, which happen to be her favorite.

Was he expecting her?

The warmth from the fire felt so good on the cold Texas winter night. The glow of the fire seemed to make Jude's golden flecks in his hazel eyes shine brighter. He had his marshmallow slowly roasting, and he was every so often rotating it.

Laynie adjusted her grip and stuck the stick straight into the hottest part of the flames. Barely any time passed before the entire thing was ablaze.

She pulled the marshmallow towards her face and softly blew, extinguishing the fire consuming her marshmallow. What was left was a crunchy black shell that honestly looked like ash. But she knew it would be ooey gooey on the inside.

Jude shook his head slowly at her, in disbelief, with a small smile on his face.

"What? You got a problem with my marshmallow?" Laynie questioned, stubbornness shining like the fire between them.

She pulled the black shell of a marshmallow off, did a quick test to make sure she wouldn't burn herself, and took a large bite. The cream inside tasted so good, even though she knew it was probably all over her face.

Now, Jude had a full out grin on his face. "You just don't like to wait for anything, do you?"

Laynie wiped her mouth with the sleeve of her hoodie, before answering, "Why wait, when I can have exactly what I want right now?" She smirked, fully aware of her flirtatious tone. Would he flirt back? Would she run back to her bed, embarrassed and alone forever?

Jude sat quietly for a moment, which drove Laynie crazy. He was just there, slowly rotating that damn marshmallow. Letting all sides get a toasty golden brown, before finally pulling it out and giving it a soft blow.

Laynie was full on staring at his lips.

Jude held eye contact, but still didn't say anything. Laynie started almost shaking, from nerves, or from something else...

He finally spoke, almost whispering, "You see, darlin', sometimes the waiting is the best part." He closed his eyes then and ate the marshmallow right off the stick. He kept his eyes closed, savoring in the moment.

Laynie was transfixed, almost wishing either she could taste the marshmallow or maybe she wished she could be the marshmallow. She definitely was feeling the heat from the fire now.

As he slowly swallowed, only then did Jude finally open his eyes, locked on Laynie.

"When you finally do get what you want, after all the time spent waiting, makes it so much more satisfying." He smirked at her, which was both her favorite and most aggravating face of his. The way his mouth was lifted just on one side, showing off a dimple hidden amongst his scruff. She just wanted to slap the smirk right off his face. Or kiss his dimple...one of those things.

Laynie shook herself. She cannot get all swoony-eyed over this man right now. She needs sleep to make a conscientious decision, not one brought about by raging hormones and sugar.

"I'm just going to walk around the house and head to bed. I need to get some sleep...see you in the morning?" She smiled at him while standing up, setting down the metal stick. He stood up then, as if to stop her.

"Wait, um, let me walk you?" He asked, a hopeful glint in his eyes.

"To the door that is literally twenty feet away? Thanks, but no thanks. I can take care of myself, Jude." She patted him appreciatively on the arm before walking back towards the house. Admiring the stars in the sky and the Christmas lights lighting up the house, Laynie was in awe of everything around her. Plus a little love drunk if you ask me.

She was so distracted, not looking right in front of her, it wasn't until she heard Zoe bark from inside the house that she realized something was wrong.

She jerked her head to her left, facing the woods. She gasped, frozen in her tracks.

The coyote was right there, staring at her, and it was moving closer with each step.

Blood lined its lips, the coyote had already had one snack tonight.

It was looking at its next one.

Chapter 8

Laynie was terrified.

She couldn't remember what to do if you run in to a coyote. Do you get tall?? Do you freeze since they only will chase you if you run? Do you make a lot of noise?

Was that for bears or coyotes? Laynie forgot everything she learned in her three weeks of Girl Scouts. Being a lover of the farm did not mean she loved everything about the wilderness.

Laynie was still struggling with what to do when suddenly she heard, "YODELLL-LEYYY-HEEEE- WHOOOO!" Followed by a, "Ay Yi Yi Yi Yah!"

The coyote stopped in its tracks and ran back towards the woods.

Laynie whipped around back to the direction of the bonfire.

Jude was standing up, and then he closed the distance between them.

Suddenly, he was right in front of her, holding her hands.

"Are you okay?" He was inches from her face, worry in his eyes. He also still hadn't let go of her hands.

Laynie looked down at their joined hands, then back up at him. "Did you just yodel?" She asked in disbelief.

"Ha. Yes I did."

"Wha- I mean, was that a- Why are you-" Laynie sighed. Clearly, the time for coherent thinking had passed.

Jude smiled and brought their joined hands to his chest, pulling her in a bit tighter, as if to make sure she was physically okay. "Well, it worked, didn't it, darlin'?"

He then shocked the tar out of her; he brought her hands to his lips. He gently brushed his lips across the tops of her knuckles. He slowly brought her hands back to her side.

Laynie felt her mouth drop about an inch.

First, sexual innuendos with marshmallows, then yodeling at a coyote, now he is kissing her knuckles?!

"Hey! Wait a minute, were you following me back home?" She suddenly realized with a start. Though to be honest, she was glad he did.

"Yep." He sighed for a moment, as if gathering how to put into words what he was feeling. He looked up at the stars as if they were giving him the answers. He continued, "I know you say you can take care of yourself, Laynie Marie, but what if I want to take care of you?" What is she supposed to say to that? How can he make her feel two different things all at once- enraged and mystified.

"Well...um, thank you for um, yodeling I suppose." Laynie stammered out.

"My pleasure." The smirk was back.

"Um-Er. Uh, well, goodnight then." Laynie then bolted back to the house before she could embarrass herself any further.

She sprinted all the way to room as quietly as she could, shut her door, and pressed her back against it, breathless.

Zoe popped up and cocked her head, questioning.

"Don't you even start, Zo Bo." Laynie quickly took off her cold weather clothes, and without letting herself dwell on what just happened, she got into bed and fell asleep.

Surprisingly, Laynie slept well. Guess getting almost attacked by a coyote will guarantee a good night's sleep?

Zoe was asking to be let out, so Laynie shrugged on some clothes quickly and opened the door.

Laynie followed her out, looking sheepishly around. She decided something waking up this morning.

She was going to get some answers today.

Now to just get the questions out...

She walked in the kitchen after letting Zoe outside. She did a quick look around much to her disappointment, no Jude.

Memaw was busy in the kitchen like always- "What's happening, sweetheart?" She turned to peek over her shoulder at Laynie then went back to her mixing bowl.

"Um, Have you seen Jude this morning, Memaw?" Laynie quietly asked.

Memaw smiled to herself, never taking her eyes off the bowl- like this had been her plan all along.

"He's spraying vinegar around the perimeter outside, supposed to repel coyotes. I heard y'all had a scare last night. I guess coyotes are attracted to marshmallows..." Her voice trailed off.

Laynie's eyebrows shot up. Either Jude had blabbed, or the more likely answer is that Memaw was spying last night.

Sneaky sneakster.

The wassail was brewing on the stove, with the oranges floating around. The citrus cinnamon smell filled up Laynie's senses, the perfect smell of Christmas.

"I'm going to bring Jude a cup of wassail. It's cold outside." She grabbed two mugs, and ladled a good helping in each.

"Sure, honey, that's nice." Memaw said, quietly, a grin appearing on her face. Memaw may be the mastermind...

Laynie carefully opened the door, and balanced the cups in her hand. The smell of vinegar combined with the smell of the wassail. She looked around for Jude, went all the way around the property before finally finding his signature flannel over by the cabin. He was spraying around the cabin, leaving no patch of dried grass uncovered.

Between his yodeling and his vinegar, the coyote didn't stand a chance.

Laynie quickly controlled herself before letting her smile show- it was time to be serious, she was on a mission after all.

"Jude- put down the vinegar and back away, we need to talk." Laynie handed him his wassail mug, and he took it with a quick thanks, looking a little surprised to see her.

Laynie took a deep breath. Of course she was confronting him at the scene of the crime. The cabin was there right behind him, daring her to chicken out.

"So, ahem, I think its safe to say there is something between us. Don't you dare deny it, mister, I know you would do that just to mess with me." She had her finger up, stopping him. He snickered to himself as if that had been exactly his plan. He then gestured for her to continue, knowing she was far from done.

"Before I even allow this thought of a possibility between us, I need answers, Jude." The tone turned serious, Jude's smile dropped and he looked at the ground in shame.

"I know you do, Laynie." Jude sighed, not looking at her. It took all the patience she possessed in her not to push him for answers.

Something she had tried to work on as an adult was patience...she still didn't have much, but she knew she needed to give him time. She waited, trying to keep her impatience from showing externally. Her toes were tapping inside her shoes anxiously, hopefully he couldn't see it.

"I loved you so much, Laynie. I think I have loved you since the first day I met you, and you proposed to me." He smiled at the memory before continuing- "I always thought love was all you needed. So, when we went to college, and everyone else broke up out of precaution, I thought they just were weak. Their love just wasn't strong enough like ours was." Laynie felt her eyes start to fill, knowing she thought the same thing back then.

"But life was hard, and I wasn't able to function then. I know I hurt you, but I hurt myself too." He finally took his eyes off the ground and saw he was crying. Slow tears were running down his scruffy cheeks. Somehow this made everything hurt so much more for Laynie.

"Honestly, that whole situation made me take a hard look at myself. How could I just cheat on you like that? How could I just drop out of school? How could I go from being the most dependable, loyal man, to the one who ruined everything? I knew I was flushing my life down the drain, and I just didn't want to drag you down more than I already had."

He took a shaky inhale, readying himself for more, keeping his eyes locked on Laynie. "I knew there was something wrong with me. So, I started therapy. I was living here, and would drive an hour twice a week to see my therapist. After about six months, my therapist suggested medication." Laynie perked up, questioning him silently.

"I know, I know." He said, both hands up as in surrender. "My initial reaction was a hell no. But then I thought of how much I had hurt the people I cared about, how much I had hurt you, and then it was easier to agree to." Laynie couldn't help it then, she reached for his hand. No matter where they would end up, she wanted him to know she always will be there for him. She would have been there for him then too. But, she knows he didn't want to burden her with his mess.

"It hasn't been easy. But probably the past five years, I finally have had a handle on my mental health, and figured out what works best for me with my medication. Honestly the thing that helped the most...coming back here." He paused and looked around, nature seeming to stop around him as if to listen to his words.

"I tried the city, I have been all over Texas and tried other places too. But nothing felt like home. Everything just makes sense here. Did you know my parents only live here about three months total out of the year? They like city luxury, but they keep this place for me." He smiled, a sense of pride showing on his face. "But I don't just work for your Memaw, I do work for properties all within an hour radius of here. I now have become a hot commodity in these parts."

Laynie agreed whole heartedly.

"Your Pepaw changed my life, Laynie."

Great, tears again.

"He called me up out of the blue when I was feeling a bit lost. He said, 'Boy, you need to come back home.'" Jude cleared his throat, struggling to finish. "You still have things you need to learn, and I still got some more stuff to teach."

"That was a couple years ago. It started off as an apprenticeship of sorts, and he taught me all sorts of things. From what bugs are okay to eat, to how to listen to what nature is trying to tell you. Laynie, I can hear it all." He closed his eyes, listening to the sounds starting back up.

"I know it's not fair to you that I am here. I know Memaw is your grandma and Pepaw was your grandpa, and this is not my property. But this...it's my home."

Laynie opened her mouth to say something- but he stopped her.

"I know I should have reached out years ago, I just was terrified of hurting you again. Even now, I am terrified. I am terrified of how much I love you."

"I know you have a life four hours away. You seem happy. I just wanted to shoot my shot with the girl I haven't stopped thinking about for twenty-five years."

Laynie waited, making sure he was finally done, eyebrows lifted. He gestured towards her, indicating the floor was now hers.

She took a breath before saying, "I'm not."

He paused, confused. "You're not, what?"

"I'm not happy. I hate my job. I feel lost without Pepaw, and other than Zoe, I haven't had a healthy relationship my entire life. Plus...she's a dog, so I am not sure it counts."

"It counts, go on." Jude said, with a grin.

"Well, even before all this with you, I was thinking about relocating. Staying here with Memaw so she's not alone. But, that was before I knew you were here."

"And now you know I'm here?" He asked, a touch of longing in his voice.

"Now, I have to stay." Laynie grinned,

Jude stood completely still for a moment, Laynie wasn't sure he heard her.

Then, he let out a "Whooop!" Scaring all the birds that were nearby, then Jude put his hands underneath Laynie's arms, picking her up and spinning her around.

The giggles came out then, and in this moment, they both were truly happy.

They were both covered in lukewarm wassail, smelled like vinegar, and had huge grins on their faces by the time they made it back inside the kitchen.

Sneaky matchmaker Memaw was stirring a pot on the stove, acting as though she hadn't seen the whole ordeal out the tiny kitchen window above the sink.

With a big smile on her face, she turned towards Laynie and Jude and asked, "Hey, you two, what's new?"

Chapter 9

Christmas Time

Laynie blinked and it was Christmas Eve. Laynie and Memaw spent the day in the kitchen, while Jude was off working on some secret project of his. Wouldn't speak a word of it to Laynie, very hush, hush.

Laynie was so happy, she even offered to clove the oranges for the fresh wassail. Not even malicious cloves would ruin her good mood.

The past few days with Jude was like no time had passed, picking up right where they had left off ten years ago. But in another sense, they also were whole people now. Grown adults who knew their wants, and they actually were mature versus when they were horny teenagers.

Now, they were horny adults.

Laynie couldn't keep her hands off of Jude. Even Memaw had to clear her throat a few times when the two of them would get a bit too handsy. But Memaw, not so secretly, loved the two of them together.

Other than a few stolen kisses outside, and some vigorous petting, and let's be real, a few booty smacks, from Laynie to Jude, of course, the new (not really new) couple couldn't be together like they truly wanted to be.

That was *very* frustrating.

So, Laynie had thrown herself into Christmas mode, since she couldn't throw herself at Jude.

Halls-Decked. Stockings- Hung with care. She even made a surprise ornament for her siblings, her mom, and Memaw.

Laynie had snuck one of Pepaw's shirts out of the closet. Actually, it was a shirt she remembers him wearing often. Without Memaw knowing, she rounded up some mason jar lids and cut Pepaw's shirt into perfect circles. She then glued the shirt piece on the circular lid, screwing the ring part of the lid over it. To finish, she glued a red ribbon on the edge of the lid, bringing in the Christmas colors. Lastly, she secured twine around the edge, ready to hang up on the tree.

She made herself one too, even though her and Jude hadn't fully discussed what was next for them. Would she even have a place to hang it? But one thing she knew, they would be together. They just didn't know where just yet.

Laynie still had her family's presents with her, even though she wasn't sure when they were exchanging gifts.

Laynie was the only childless adult, and they each had their own families to do Christmas with. Laynie would be the Santa Claus as soon as she went back home. She absolutely loved spoiling her nieces and nephews.

But she was missing her parents. Being the baby, she still spent Christmas with her parents every year. This would be her first Christmas without them.

But...Laynie's mom knew when she pushed Laynie to go to Memaw's, that would mean they wouldn't get to spend Christmas together.

Laynie had already planned on FaceTiming her mom and dad later today. Making sure they had on their Christmas pajamas that she had already given them before she left to wear on Christmas Eve.

She wondered what her parents would think about Jude. They had loved him growing up, but when he broke her heart they had publicly disowned him. However, Laynie knew for a fact that her mom still sent him Christmas cards every single year, and that both her parents were facebook friends with him.

Her mom would be thrilled, she had done her granddaughter duty, and gained a boyfriend all in one trip.

Her dad would be a little more wary...He was the practical one, while her mom was the dreamer. He would be asking all the hard questions that her and Jude were currently avoiding.

"So, What's the plan here?"

"Where will y'all live?"

"Are you quitting your job?"

"Jude, what exactly is your job?"

"Are you getting married?"

"Will you have kids?"

Laynie was worried that those types of questions would destroy the little stability their relationship had. She knew Jude's mental health isn't something that just gets better, it's a constant journey. Would the two of them together just bring everything back that caused them to split the first time?

No. She wouldn't allow that to happen.

Laynie also had already decided, she had spent too much time in her life without Jude. Laynie would spend as much time with him as she could. Even if he broke her heart again in a few years, or they only have three month together, those three months would be worth it.

She hoped.

Now for her next dilemma of the day...what to give Jude for Christmas.

Since Memaw had surprised her with his presence, she hadn't packed him a present. So, she had to come up with one extremely last minute.

Laynie knew if anyone could create a spectacular present for reunited childhood sweethearts, it was her. She was a crafty queen, after all. The family ornaments honoring Pepaw, Exhibit A. The bandana around Zoe's neck currently that said, 'Santa Paws', Exhibit B. The freaking Christmas tree garland she had put together herself instead of spending hundreds of dollars buying it premade, Exhibit C.

Not getting inspired by anything inside, Laynie took her search outside. She tried to get Zoe to come, but Zo Bo was currently getting all the scraps that made it to the floor while Memaw was cooking, AKA Pup Heaven. Laynie wasn't sure exactly where Jude was, but wherever he was, she hoped he stayed extremely focused on his task for the time being. She had a present to make.

The forest surrounded the house, but there was a single tree inside the house line. It was a magnolia tree, and Laynie had been obsessed with it her whole life. Jude used to pluck a flower from the tree and stick it in her hair.

"Beautiful," he would say.

"Thank you," She would smile sweetly, acting as if she didn't know what would come next.

"I meant the flower, silly." Jude would say, and then he would spend the next few minutes dodging her playful hits and tickles from her.

The tree never failed to bloom, even though it was older than she was, and she used to make a special trip to see the magnolias blooming. While it wasn't currently in bloom, it still was beautiful. Though the cliche part of her, really wanted to carve out their initials in the tree to commemorate their relationship, she knew Pepaw would hate it and would probably haunt her if she hurt his tree like that.

Maybe there was something around the tree she could use...

She walked around, careful to avoid the many bugs surrounding the tree trunk. Finally, she saw it- the perfect tool for her gift to Jude.

One of the thicker branches was at the base of the tree and it was about three inches wide in diameter, and about four feet tall. It was relatively smooth, which made her job easier, and the only separating smaller branches were at the very top. Laynie ran to the garage with her prize, afraid of being caught by Jude.

Good ole Pepaw- coming through for her even now. Everything she needed was within hand's reach. He had a whole wall of tools she could use, and she even saw sander paper, and wood stain all on his work counter.

Laynie checked her watch- Memaw had said Jude and her were expected at dinner by six, and it was currently 2:00. She had some work to do.

Chapter 10

Laynie was covered in wood chips, had a couple of splinters, and was stained with wood stain, but Jude's gift was done.

She had made him a beautiful walking stick- and as a bonus, she had carved their initials right below the handle. That way, no matter the living situation or what came next, he would always have a reminder of her, of them.

She showered quickly, trying to get the stain and wood shavings all off. Laynie felt scrubbed raw by the time she left the shower. She checked her watch, ten minutes to spare. She still had to put on some makeup, which wouldn't take long since she always went a little light, dry her hair, and put on her Christmas Eve pajamas.

Right after dinner, she was going to call her parents to make sure they had their set on too.

Laynie quickly finished getting ready, managing to do it all within the ten minute mark, arriving to the kitchen right at six o'clock on the dot. Most of her friends back home took hours to get ready, but she had always prided herself on her speed and efficiency.

Memaw, who Laynie knew had been in the kitchen all last night and today, looked fresh and happy, not tired and grumpy like Laynie would have been. But Memaw got so much joy from cooking and taking care of others, so even though Laynie had a comfy, cozy, present waiting under the tree for Memaw, the best thing she did for her Memaw was come see her. Jude loved eating Memaw's cooking, but he also was so low maintenance, he barely ate one sit down meal a day. Memaw missed Pepaw, of course, but she missed the joy she got from taking care of someone she loved. Memaw loved the joy people got from her food, and felt joy by giving others joy. Pepaw always used to joke he married Memaw for her cooking, but anyone who saw the two of them together, it was clear. The two of them loved each other with their whole souls for over sixty years, and Laynie had always longed for a love that came close to theirs. She always thought she had missed her chance for love, though.

Jude walked through the door, and a huge grin appeared on Laynie's face. Jude looked handsome as always, his beard trimmed for the occasion, his hair fixed for once, the light smell of cologne mixing in with the wassail aroma from the kitchen. But that's not what made Laynie smile, Jude was decked out head to toe in his very own Christmas pajamas.

Why did Laynie suddenly want to start crying?

"Shake it off, Laynie, you got a whole Christmas dinner to get through, there's no time for crying." Laynie thought to herself, before walking over to her crush she had had for twenty-five years.

"Hey, you." Jude said, smiling down at Laynie.

"Hey, yourself, cowboy. Looking good, Jude." Laynie said, reaching for his hands.

He looked down at their joined hands, shaking his head in disbelief. "I can't believe we got here, Lay. I am so happy right now, I feel like I must be dreaming. But I am perfectly happy on staying asleep if that's the case." He kissed her cheek, both his words and his kiss making color come to her cheeks, then he led her to the kitchen table. Jude pulled out her chair, waiting for her to sit, before joining her in the chair next to her.

Memaw started setting up the table, putting down five placemats, five plates, five glass cups and five silverware settings.

Laynie looked up at Memaw, questioning, "Expecting company, Memaw?" Memaw shared a look with Jude, and then the two shared a mischievous smile.

Laynie was just about to ask what they were up to, when suddenly, there was a knock at the door.

"Just in time," Memaw said, opening up the door right by the table.

Holding open the screen door, clad in their matching Christmas pajamas, were Laynie's mom and dad.

"Mom! Dad! You're here!" Laynie ran over to greet her parents as they stepped inside.

"Merry Christmas, Laynie Marie." Her parents both wrapped their arms around her, and she was sandwiched between the two.

"How are y'all here?" Laynie asked in disbelief as she finally pulled away from her parents.

"Jude called us the day you came down and planned the whole thing." Laynie's mom said with a knowing smile. She raised her eyebrows at Laynie suggestively. Laynie chose to ignore her mother and turned towards Jude, who was standing by his seat over at the table.

"Jude? You called them?"

"Yep, he did. Plus, I knew the whole time!" Memaw said triumphantly, proud of herself for keeping it a secret. Everyone giggled and then got settled in for dinner.

Well, that explains the feast Memaw had been preparing. Roasted turkey, stuffing, vegetarian dressing, green bean casserole, sweet potato casserole, macaroni and cheese, plus of course, the desserts. Laynie's snickerdoodles, pumpkin dump cake, blueberry cream pie, and chocolate cream pie. Memaw even made a mini pecan pie, in honor of Pepaw. Laynie's mom was the one who ate it, since pecan was her favorite too. Even though this was the first Christmas without Pepaw, he was everywhere.

He was in the laughs they shared when Laynie told the coyote yodeling story. He was a part of the food they had, as they struggled to loosen their pants after "just one more bite". Finally, he was present in the love they all shared with one another as they talked about how grateful they were for each other.

Jude wiped a tear from his eye, Laynie caught his hand and brought it to her lips. She then pulled it to rest in her lap.

"I am so thankful for you all, truly." Jude said, voice wavering slightly.

"Hey, bud. That's my line." Memaw said playfully before continuing. "Laynie, Jude, you have made what could have been the worst Christmas, truly magical. I was dreading being...alone this year. But I have you all with me, and I know with all of my heart," Memaw placed her hand to her chest. "Your Pepaw is here with us."

Now, Laynie was the one wiping a tear off of her cheek.

Looking around the dinner table, Memaw had successfully brought everyone to tears. "Hush now, y'all, it's Christmas. Santa only comes once everyone is asleep." So, everyone said their good nights and Laynie's parents got settled in her room. Laynie gave Zoe a last cuddle for the night, then went into the living room to settle in on the couch.

Laynie jumped out of her skin when she saw Jude standing beneath the glow of the Christmas tree. "Jude! You gave me a heart attack! What on earth are you doing creepily standing in the dark?"

Jude chuckled and reached for her hand, "Ready for your Christmas present, Lay?"

Laynie paused, hesitating to grab Jude's hand. She thought of the reasons they broke up the first time. How he had cheated on her all those years ago. But she also thought how he had single handedly been helping her grandparents the past few years. How he always puts others first, before himself. How he knew she would want her parents here for Christmas, and did everything in his power to bring them here. He even wore Christmas pajamas because he had remembered it was one of her favorite Christmas traditions, and he wanted to be a part of it.

"More than ready, Jude." Laynie said grabbing his outstretched hand.

Chapter 11

Jude quietly led Laynie out of the house, into the night.

"Okay, seriously, where are we going? You'd tell me if the present was my murder, right?" Laynie joked, halfway serious. The woods made everything ten times scarier.

"One- of course I wouldn't tell you. Two- What if Mr. Coyote had his own plans for you tonight?" Jude avoided her question about their whereabouts and just kept leading towards his surprise.

"Ughh.. Shut up! He could be listening!" Laynie playfully smacked his arm, but she still followed him into the trees. Laynie realized she would follow this man anywhere...

After a few more steps, she finally figured out where he was leading her- the cabin.

First off, she wasn't sure how she missed it, but Jude had added white Christmas lights around the tin roof of the cabin. He also had mirrored her garland around the house and made it at a much smaller scale, and he had framed it around the door frame.

For someone who always had something to say, Laynie was speechless.

"Come on, there's more inside." Jude said, leading her in the gated porch. The magic didn't stop once she stepped in. He had gotten a miniature Christmas tree and decorated it with tiny framed pictures throughout their childhood. One was the same picture Memaw had on the piano, another was from when they were older and on the four wheeler together, Laynie's arms wrapped around Jude's waist. There were about ten pictures, all from some of Laynie's favorite moments. There even was a recent picture, that Memaw must have snagged the other day. The two of them looking at each other and laughing. Even though Laynie didn't remember what they must have been talking about, its clear from the picture that they still loved one another. She knew it, but to have photographic evidence staring her in the face made it obvious.

Jude also had gotten new bedding for the tiny twin bed. It was still tiny, but now it actually looked cozy and cushiony, unlike it was before. The bedding was red and blue plaid, which reminded Laynie of Jude's signature flannel, and the pillows were solid red, like the sheets.

"Merry Christmas, Lay." Jude said from behind her. She turned towards him, and saw he had somehow snuck in two travel mugs.

"Wassail?" She asked, reaching for the mug.

'Wassail." He smiled, agreeing. They each took and sip and sat on the edge of the bed, not quite looking at one another.

The wassail was delicious like always, citrusy and warm down the throat, and the bed was so much better than before. Laynie wondered if Jude had added a memory foam topper, that would explain the extra plushness. Laynie started looking around the tiny cabin, everywhere except to her left. He had fixed up the cabin with little tweaks here and there, she noticed. This wasn't just a one day job, he had been working on this a long time, she realized. When she couldn't avoid it any longer, she looked at him. At the same time, he turned towards her.

"I-" She said.

"We-er". They both spoke at same time. Jude gestured at Laynie to go ahead and said, "Ladies first."

"Okay." Laynie took a breath. "Here's the deal. I want to be with you. Whether it's here or we move to my apartment, or we move to Alaska. I do not care. I want to be with you. I will even try long distance again if that's what you want." Laynie said barely taking a breath.

She waited five seconds for his response before saying breathlessly, "Say something!"

He smiled and said, "I love you, Laynie Marie. Heck, Alaska works for me." Jude laughed as she groaned, annoyed, and hit his arm.

As soon as her hand make contact, he reached for her hand and pulled it to his cheek, pulling her in and forcing them an inch apart. Laynie could feel his breath tickling her eye lashes, she wanted to blink, but was afraid to break the connection between them.

Time seemed to slow down in this moment. Neither one of them moving, just frozen, locked in on each other's eyes. Laynie was the first to move, bringing the hand that was on Jude's cheek to the back of his neck. She stayed there a moment, waiting to see if he would move. Then, she pulled him in, her lips crashing to his.

He moved then, giving into the kiss, coming alive. He slid her backside onto his lap, opening up his legs to allow her to come in closer. Neither one of them broke the kiss, not even to come up for air. Laynie had both hands around his neck and then ran her fingers through his hair, causing him to shiver.

He broke apart then, pulling away ever so slightly to look into her hooded eyes, and said, "I can't get enough of you. I have so much to make up for, Laynie." Then he pulled them both down on the bed, side by side laying down.

He moved in to kiss her again, but she stopped him and said, "Wait, covers!" He smirked and said, "Don't worry, baby, I'll get you warm." Then, his large body, still fully clad in Christmas pajamas, climbed on top of her, closing her in her own personal furnace. She relaxed deeper into the pillow, as his kisses traveled down her neck. She forced her self not to move, even though all she wanted to do was touch him and travel her hands down his muscular back. Both her and Jude would have more fun the longer she waited to touch him...

He kissed all down her neck, her clavicle where the buttons on her Christmas pj top began, and he lifted the bottom of her shirt to lightly kiss her lower belly. Jude's eyes then looked up at her wickedly, before reaching to lower her shorts.

She went to stop him, knowing what his intentions were. "Wait, what about you, Jude? I want *you*." Her hands reached for his cheek, forcing his head back up to look at her.

He gently pushed her hands back into the bed, holding them in place, and said, "Baby, we got all the time in the world. Right now, I am giving you your Christmas present, so hush."

Laynie listened and hushed up, until she couldn't be quiet anymore...

Hours later, into the middle of the early morning, the two finally fell still, wrapped in each others arms. They were cozy and comfy in the tiniest of beds.

Laynie knew sleep was about to take her, both mind and body spent, but she said just before she fell asleep, "Merry Christmas, Jude."

"Merry Christmas, Lay. Now, get some sleep, or Santa won't come." Jude said with a smile, closing his eyes himself. Laynie nuzzled in closer to Jude, thinking she wasn't sure life could get better than this.

If either one of them would have had their eyes open in that moment, they would have seen a coyote peeking though the cabin window for just a moment, before traveling on to a less smelly destination.

Chapter 12

One Year Later

It was Christmas again in the country, but this time the whole gang was there. Laynie's parents, all of Laynie's siblings and their families, Jude's parents, and of course, Zoe.

Laynie's siblings' and their kids stayed at Jude's parents house with them. Laynie's parents stayed in Laynie's old room, and Laynie and Jude stayed in the cabin, for old time's sake. Zoe would float from room to room, not wanting anyone to think they were the favorite. She would give cuddles to anyone, much to Laynie's annoyance.

All of Laynie's nieces and nephews loved the animals, though the littlest ones needed some encouragement when it came to feeding the cows. When the cow's giant mouth comes at a little hand, it can be a bit frightening.

They got to do activities together that Laynie and her siblings hadn't done since they were kids. They all took turns on the four wheeler, hearing their Pepaw's warnings about taking turns too fast, and not speeding over the bridge. They all cuddled up together by the fire, roasting marshmallows. Laynie avoided Jude's eyes the whole night, not able to control her blushing thinking of last year. And of course, everyone enjoyed dish after dish of Memaw's cooking.

In fact, this year, Laynie started a new tradition. Baking with Aunt Lay- where all of her nieces and nephews would help her bake cookies for Santa and different baked goods for the whole family. It was definitely crazy, especially with the toddlers running around covered in sugar and flour, but Laynie loved every second of it. Luckily, Jude was there to help with the biggest messes, while every other adult just stood back and watched the chaos unfold.

Laynie wondered if her own kids would help her in the kitchen one day...

Laynie and Jude had been splitting their time back and forth between the farm and her apartment. Memaw loved that she got to see Laynie so much. Luckily, Zoe's motion sickness had gotten so much better after so much car time between her two homes. Jude would find work in the city when they were at Laynie's. He was so good at everything, he had developed a sort of cult following with his renovation work that people jumped on any opportunity he was there. Laynie kept her job, but had started enforcing a few ground rules so that businesses wouldn't take advantage of her. They needed a counselor on call for the workers she talked to, *and* they needed to warn her if there was a potentially difficult conversation. She also reserved the right to end any call that would become hazardous to her mental well being. Her clients were wary at first at her new ground rules, but when she threatened to quit, they agreed whole heartedly.

While they managed to make it work, back and forth was not ideal for Jude, Laynie, or Zoe. So, they had decided a few months back, they would move to the country. That way, Jude could still keep an eye on his parent's house, since they were barely there, and still work for Memaw and all the other country clients.

There was land that backed up to Memaw's property that they wanted to build their very own house on. It was a labor of love and would take months before it would be ready, but until then, Memaw said they always had the cabin if they wanted it.

"It may be tiny," she said, "But it sure is cozy."

The last night at Memaw's for everyone was Christmas Eve, everyone would be going back to their own homes after presents Christmas morning. Even Laynie was going back to her apartment for a bit to get some packing started for the move coming up. Jude was staying behind to get Christmas packed up at Memaw's. They didn't like it, but they were going to be spending New Year's apart.

After a night of hot cocoa, Christmas pajamas, wassail, marshmallows, and Pepaw stories told around the fire, everyone went their separate ways to bed.

Laynie and Jude held hands as they made their way to their tiny cabin.

"That was fun," Laynie said, looking up at Jude, his eyes glowing from the Christmas lights around them.

"It was. It was good to have everyone here together, doesn't happen often." Jude said, squeezing Laynie's hand as the cabin came into view.

"But I'm glad it can be just us now. I want you all to myself." Laynie wrapped her arms around Jude, squeezing him before reaching to open the cabin door.

"Back at ya, baby. I'm glad we get one night, just us, since it'll be a bit until our next one." Jude agreed, putting down their to-go travel mugs. His had cocoa this time and hers had wassail in it; she had just downed the cup on the way over.

"Pretty soon though, every night can be just us...". Laynie said with a smile, climbing under the covers. She was thinking of the dream house they had started working on, the design was a perfect mix of his rustic and her country/city combo, and she could not wait til they were in it together. Next Christmas, they would be in their own home, with their own decorations, but they would still help Memaw with hers of course.

"Hey, Laynie?" Jude asked, as he fiddled with his bag over on the table.

"What's up, Jude?" Laynie peeked out from underneath the covers to see what he was fiddling with.

Jude, still in his matching Christmas pajamas of the year, dropped down on one knee in their tiny cabin, much to Laynie's surprise, and asked, "Want to play husbands and wives with me?"

Best Christmas Ever.

Author's Note

Never did I think I would write a holiday romance, since I have always been a fantasy girlie- it definitely was a challenge, but it also was so fun. I loved writing this book for the same reason I love fantasy, it's a way to escape.

Who knows? Maybe my next book will be a holiday romantasy... Candy Cane dragons, perhaps?

Honestly though, the best part of writing this book was incorporating the real life elements. I have a real Memaw, and her and my Pepaw used to have a farm in the country. It was my favorite place. The farm always felt magical to me as a kid, and I wanted to combine it's magic with the magic of the holiday season.

I also really did lose my Pepaw, and I wanted to write this story to honor him, but most importantly honor what he and my Memaw created together. He truly was a light in everyone's lives and those first few holidays without him were so hard on everyone.

But even though we don't have the farm anymore, I've realized the magic from the memories is still just as strong. Now, I can share those stories of Memaw and Pepaw's farm and Pepaw's silly shenanigans with my husband and daughter.

Also, writing this book allowed me to have my favorite pup, Zoe again. Zoe was with me through all of my major life milestones- first apartment by myself, my marriage, first house, and the birth of my daughter. I am so glad my daughter got to meet Zoe, even if Zoe was only around for a little bit of her life. My daughter, Livvy, talks all the time about Pepaw and Zoe are playing together in heaven. I think there must be something she knows that we as grownups have trouble picturing, because after hearing her say that the first time, I fully believe that must be true. Zoe actually used to go to Memaw and Pepaw's farm, so I can picture Pepaw throwing a ball and playing fetch with my beautiful pup.

This book made me feel all the feelings- closure for my Pepaw, love for the man in my life that inspires every romantic lead, my husband, nostalgia for one of my favorite places growing up, the farm, and a sense of magic that only comes during the holidays. I hope you enjoyed reading this book- whether it made you tear up, laugh, or suddenly get a craving for a steaming cup of wassail.

I will leave you with one final thought- let yourself tell the ones you love how much you love them. I think part of the reason the holidays are so magical, is people stop and look around at all they have in their life, and are truly grateful. What if we lived like that year round? Show our love for one another in both actions *and* words? So what if its a bit cheesy, sometimes? Embrace the cheesiness, I say. Everyone loves a good, ole, cheesy Christmas movie, or book, every now and again.

Our Wassail Recipe

Apple Juice
Pineapple Juice
Lemon Juice
3 Cloved Large Oranges
Cinnamon
Ground Cloves
Honey

About the Author

Bethany Phelps Lepretre

Dance teacher and Director by day, book author by night, Bethany certainly likes to stay busy. Bethany has always loved reading and writing, and journaled every event growing up and into adulthood. Her wedding vows were full of journal entries documenting her relationship. While reading and writing has always been a huge part of her life, only recently did she decide to pursue it by self publishing a trilogy. Dreams The Complete Trilogy is Bethany's first fantasy series. Bethany cannot wait for what is next on her author journey and is so excited of what is to come. Bethany loves the beach, reading, and spending time with her family. Bethany lives in Seabrook with her husband Kegan, their daughter Livvy, and their two dogs, Traeger and Stella.

Also By Bethany Phelps Lepretre

Dreams: A Peek into the Past

Nightmares: Further into the future

Reality: The Conclusion

Dreams: The Complete Trilogy

Be Sure to Follow Bethany for the Latest Updates on Books and Events!

Instagram: @authorbethanyphelpslepretre

www.ingramcontent.com/pod-product-compliance
Lightning Source LLC
Chambersburg PA
CBHW050459110726
47899CB00003B/1011